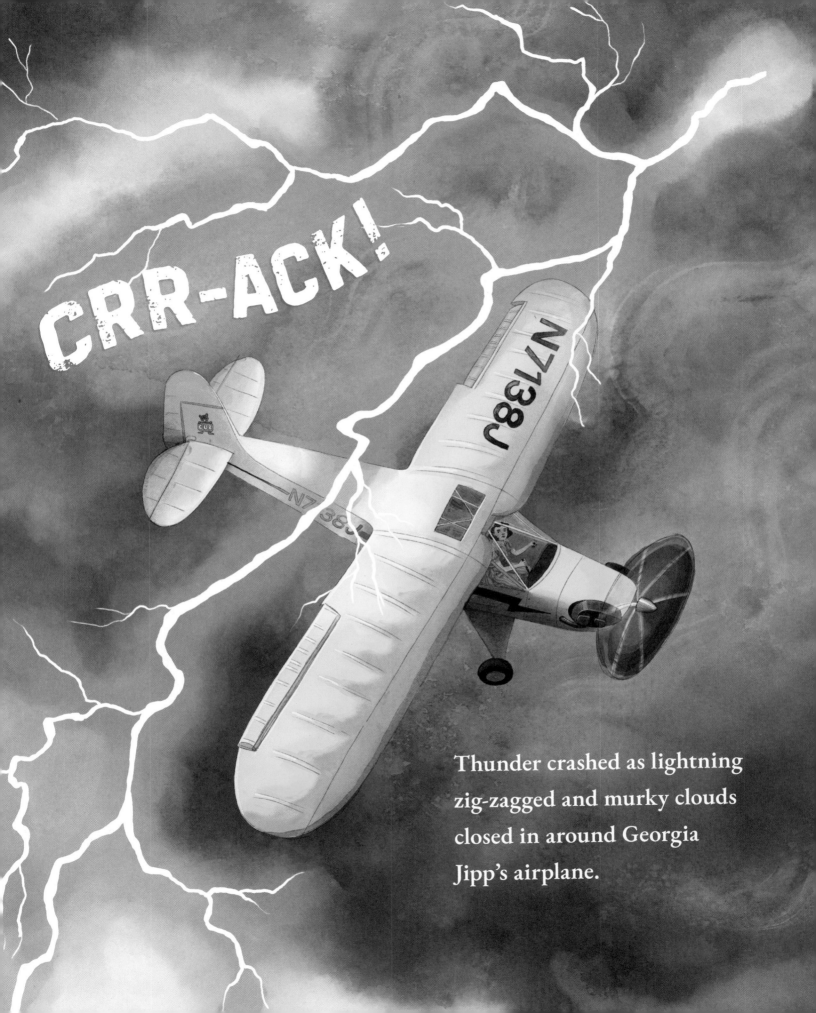

CRR-ACK!

Thunder crashed as lightning zig-zagged and murky clouds closed in around Georgia Jipp's airplane.

Torrents of rain lashed the windowpanes.
With pillows piled behind her, Georgia peered
over the nose of her plane, searching for the
makeshift runway on the open prairie.
She might be small, but she was brave.

South Dakota Historical Society Press
PIERRE

GEORGIA JIPP
BLIZZARD PILOT

Laura Beth Dean

ILLUSTRATED BY **Jeanne Bowman**

Library of Congress Cataloguing-in-Publication Data
Names: Dean, Laura Beth, author. | Bowman, Jeanne, 1988- illustrator.
Title: Georgia Jipp : blizzard pilot / Laura Beth Dean ; illustrated by Jeanne Bowman.
Description: Pierre : South Dakota Historical Society Press, [2024] |
Includes bibliographical references. | Audience: Grades 2-3 | Summary: *"Georgia Jipp: Blizzard Pilot* is about
a courageous twenty-two-year-old airplane pilot who earned her pilot's license as a teenager and risked her
life to fly mercy missions in South Dakota during the devastating winter of 1949." Provided by publisher.
Identifiers: LCCN 2024007537 | ISBN 9781941813515 (hardcover)
Subjects: LCSH: Disaster relief | Great Plains | History | 20th century. | Jipp, Georgia, 1926-1987. | Blizzards | Great Plains | History
| 20th century. | Women air pilots | South Dakota | Biography. | Air pilots | South Dakota | Biography. | Operation Snowbound, 1949.
Classification: LCC F595 .J573 2024 | DDC 51.5550978–dc23/eng/20240305

Text and cover design by Angela Corbo Gier
Editing and project management by Nancy Tystad Koupal

Photo credits: p. 20 (bottom), courtesy of Butch Amsden;
p. 21 (left) and p. 22 (left), courtesy of the American National Red Cross, all rights reserved in all countries;
p. 21 (right), courtesy of the Associated Press; p. 22 (right), courtesy of National Weather Service, Rapid City, S.Dak.

Please visit our website at www.sdhspress.com.

This publication is funded, in part, by Verna Kay Bormann, the City of Deadwood,
and the Deadwood Historic Preservation Commission.

Printed in Canada

28 27 26 25 24 1 2 3 4 5

Dedicated to my favorite flying family: Mark, Kathleen, Skyler Orion,
Zarya Christelle, and Kiana Chandelle, who inspire many to soar.

To the United States Armed Forces and their
families: thank you for your sacrifice and service!

Soli Deo gloria
— L. D.

To my family and Uncle Al — thanks for helping me fly!
— J. B.

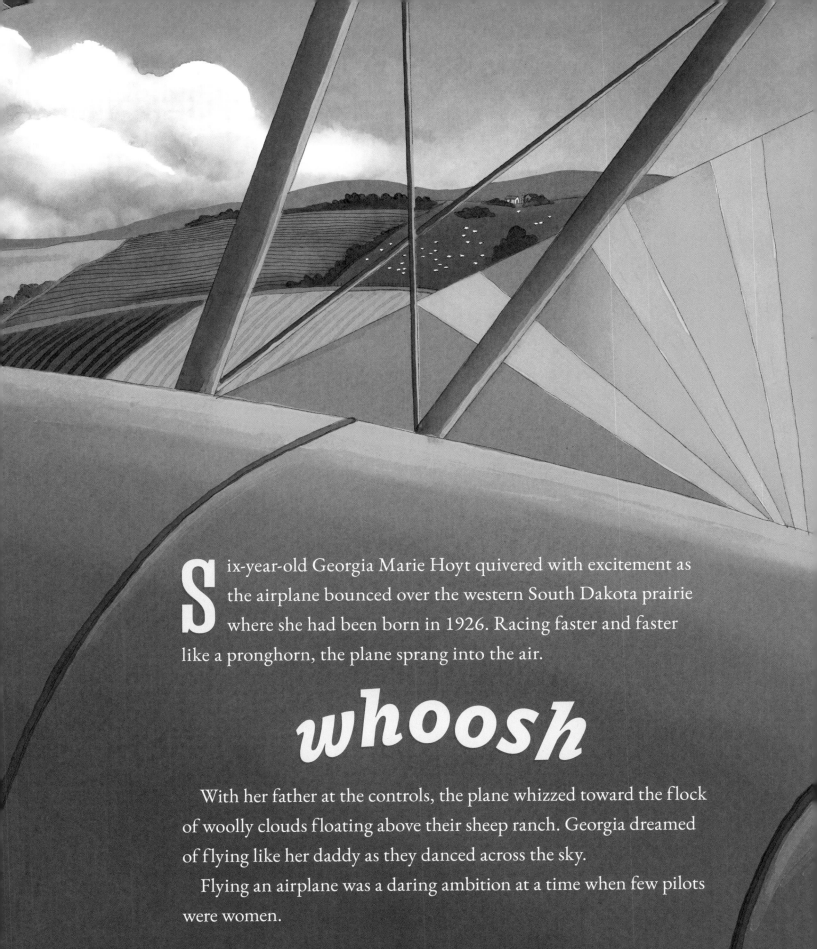

Six-year-old Georgia Marie Hoyt quivered with excitement as the airplane bounced over the western South Dakota prairie where she had been born in 1926. Racing faster and faster like a pronghorn, the plane sprang into the air.

whoosh

With her father at the controls, the plane whizzed toward the flock of woolly clouds floating above their sheep ranch. Georgia dreamed of flying like her daddy as they danced across the sky.

Flying an airplane was a daring ambition at a time when few pilots were women.

Even fewer pilots were teenage girls. But at seventeen, Georgia began flying lessons. There was just one problem. She was only five feet three inches tall.

Georgia did not let that stop her!

She nestled a pillow behind her back so she could reach the rudder pedals and brakes.

She put two pillows underneath her so she could see over the nose.

She clambered up tall stepladders to fuel the wing tanks.

When Georgia was nineteen, she earned her pilot's license.
She pirouetted her plane over the plains even when lightning
and thunder crackled across the purple sky.
She was little, but she was brave.

Georgia loved flying. When she was twenty-two, she married Richard Jipp—on an airplane!

Her mother was her matron of honor. A judge married Georgia and Richard while the airplane circled above the town of Philip.

The guests listened over the radio and cheered the couple.

The following winter, on the second day of January 1949, a blizzard veiled the western United States in white. While the wind whirled wildly, temperatures sank far below zero.

Over South Dakota, thirty-eight inches of snow spilled down in just two days. In Philip, blizzard winds howled for seventy-two hours. Snow piled up to the second-floor windows of the Senechal Hotel, stranding ranchers who had come into town for supplies. Power was out for miles.

It was the worst snowstorm in South Dakota's history.

Georgia paced back and forth in the hangar that housed her
two airplanes, a Piper Cub and an Aeronca Champ. Snowbound
people needed rides, but she was snowbound, too.

A mountain of snow rose in the middle of the runway.
Ten-foot-high drifts jammed against the hangar doors.

The telephone jangled. The ranchers pleaded with her to fly
them home. She explained that snowplows could not get through
to clear the runway.

They told her to be ready to fly in the morning. Throughout the
freezing night, the ranchers shoveled a path for Georgia's plane.

Georgia packed snowshoes and shovels and prayed as she took off. Gusts of wind pummeled her Piper Cub. The engine sputtered and threatened to die in the bitter cold.

She flew over sheep shelters, cow sheds, haystacks, houses, and schools drowning in an ocean of snow. A farmer climbed out of a high window straight onto the snow to shovel a tunnel to his door.

Georgia searched for a spot of prairie that the wind had cleared. She could not land in the snow without skis on her plane. She got the ranchers as close to their homes as she could.

She was little, but she was brave.

Snow buried roads, snapped power lines, and trapped buses and trains. Jagged snow drifts became icebergs that snowplows could not get through. Farmers ran out of food. Ranchers burned fence posts and furniture, frantic to keep warm.

Could one small pilot make a difference in this avalanche of sadness?

Georgia wanted to do all that she could, so she put skis on her Aeronca Champ. Flying a ski-plane took extra skill. Deep powder snow could swallow her plane up to its belly!

Radio stations relayed calls to Georgia. Farm families were begging for relief. From the air, Georgia searched for signs of distress that people had etched in the snow. When she spotted farm animals that had wandered over fences, she let families know where to find them. She rescued people who were lost in the endless miles of whiteness.

From dawn to dusk, through pelting snow, Georgia flew food and fuel to farms, ranches, and towns.

After each flight, Georgia's mother met her with coffee and gassed up the plane. Georgia warmed her tingling fingers before taking off again.

She was little, but she was brave.

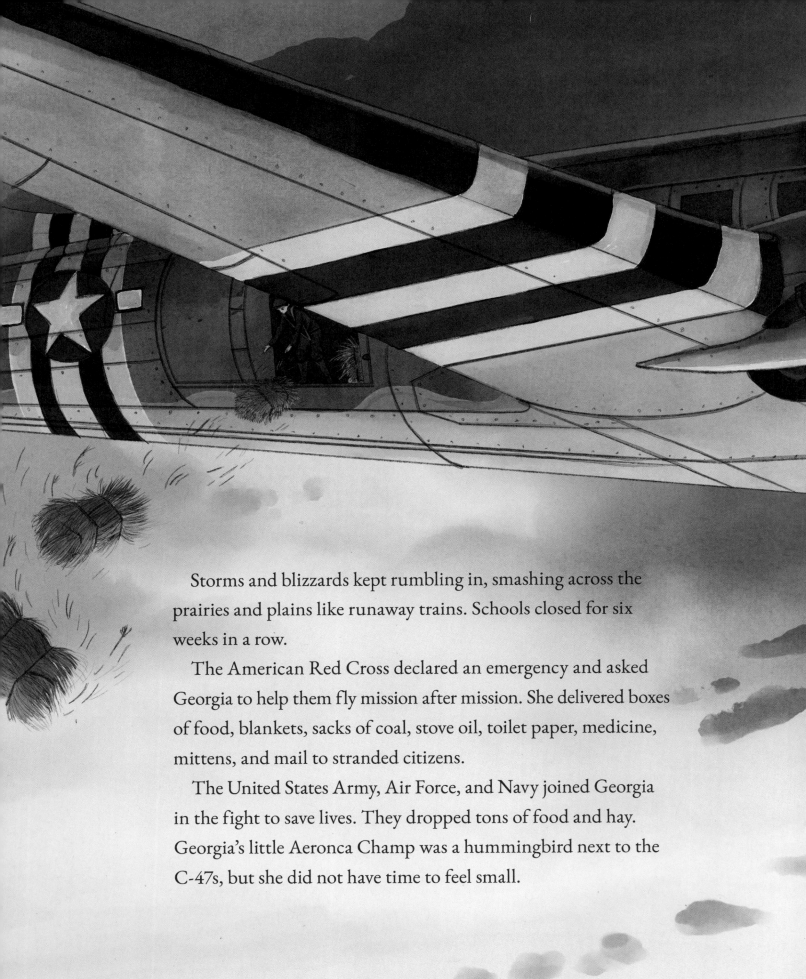

Storms and blizzards kept rumbling in, smashing across the prairies and plains like runaway trains. Schools closed for six weeks in a row.

The American Red Cross declared an emergency and asked Georgia to help them fly mission after mission. She delivered boxes of food, blankets, sacks of coal, stove oil, toilet paper, medicine, mittens, and mail to stranded citizens.

The United States Army, Air Force, and Navy joined Georgia in the fight to save lives. They dropped tons of food and hay. Georgia's little Aeronca Champ was a hummingbird next to the C-47s, but she did not have time to feel small.

When Georgia's plane suffered damage from jouncing over
jam-packed drifts, she took out her toolbox and made repairs.

When Georgia's windshield frosted inside, she turned
off the heaters, opened her window, and froze.

When Georgia's struts were stuck in crumpled clouds
of snow, she rocked and pushed to set them free.

When Georgia felt too tired to go on, she remembered the children who needed the food to stay strong and healthy. She climbed back into her plane to make yet one more delivery.

Sometimes, Georgia landed between deep feathery drifts to pick up sick children. She tucked them beneath soft feather quilts and whisked them to hospitals and then safely back home again.

At the end of March, the blizzard blitz ended with a final blow. The American Red Cross called that winter "the worst snow disaster in the history of the West."

Twenty-two-year-old Georgia Jipp had flown more than 150 mercy missions—more than anyone in South Dakota!

She was a blizzard pilot hero. No storm could stop her for long.
As Georgia sashayed her plane across the sun sweetened sky
of spring, newspapers across America praised her actions.

"**GEORGIA JIPP HAD MANY NARROW ESCAPES FROM DEATH,**"
one reporter noted.

She is "**5 FEET 3 INCHES OF PEP AND COURAGE,**" another wrote.

The Weath

Cloudy, not so cold tonight. Low
35. Snow thaw, freezing rain
tomorrow; High, 35

TWENTY-FOUR PAGES

ANGEL OF MERCY

re than 100 mercy missions to farmers and
in the vicinity of Philip for the Red Cross
first blizzard of early this month, has been
ployed by 5'3" Georgia Jipp, Philip flier.
vering food, fuel, and medical supplies to
wns and ranches, she has transported
individuals to their homes. In three
picked up people who were ill and
pitalization, returning them to Philip.
old woman, wife of one of the CAA
Philip, Richard Jipp, has also flown mail
ent emergency. The couple are well
affection for flying- having even been
e last year with her mother acting as
while guests of the couple listened
remony which was broadcasted from
n 12 Georgia flew mail from Powell
ek, a round trip of more than 100
her first flying lessons from Clyde
ishing her training at 19 in Tulsa. She
partan School of Aeronautics. She
flying instructor, charter pilot,
Hoyt flying services in Philip,
her father, Murrin Hoyt, another
At present she has logged 2,500
The young woman uses as 90
quipped with skis for her mercy
flies ... riper Cub. She is
flying for the Red Cross until
est River is relieved.

Deflates
m Broadcast

Jan 29. (AP). After
oadcast an alarm today that
tive materials had been
ret government research
Its Institute of Technology
report by stating the lost
ad bricks
ern said as a chicid in
MIT said and were only
an a foot."
tions in place to

Georgia Jipp was little and brave,
and she had made a big difference.

AUTHOR'S NOTE

It is an amazing privilege to be the first person to write a book about Georgia Jipp. I discovered her while reading Roy V. Alleman's "BLIZZARD 1949". This twenty-two-year-old pilot who risked her life and comfort to help suffering people and animals during a devastating blitz of storms inspired me, but I was disappointed to find only one other source that mentioned her. Such a hero was worthy of her own book, I thought, so I set out to write it. I searched the internet and library, wrote letters, and made phone calls.

Nobody had heard of Georgia Jipp. But I persevered and soon made exciting discoveries in newspapers and elsewhere. Eric Broussard and Amy Falkena Sundberg, Spearfish, South Dakota, librarians; Brittany Smith, administrator of the City of Philip, South Dakota; and Kate Newman, American Red Cross archive intern, also searched and found valuable pieces of information for me. Pilots Mark Navratil and Mike Navratil provided expert advice. Writing this book was a bit like building an airplane. When I had gathered a hangar full of pieces, I fit them together, riveted them with words, and painted them with imagination. Now this book is ready to fly. My hope is that the true story of Georgia Jipp will inspire you to soar.

Philip airport and hangar

Important Dates in the Life of
GEORGIA JIPP

❄ **1926** ❄

Georgia Marie Hoyt is born in Lead, South Dakota, to Murrin and Frances Hoyt on May 4.

❄ **1943** ❄

Georgia begins flight training in Spearfish, South Dakota, at age 17.

❄ **1945** ❄

She completes her training at the Spartan School of Aeronautics in Tulsa, Oklahoma, at age 19.

❄ **1946–1947** ❄

She works as a flight instructor and charter pilot for her father's business, Hoyt Flying Services in Philip, South Dakota, and then as operator of Philip Flying Service.

❄ **1948** ❄

Georgia marries Richard Jipp, a Civil Aviation Authority operator, in an airplane over Philip, on October 18.

❄ **1949** ❄

JANUARY 2–5
A blizzard devastates the Upper Great Plains. Georgia, her father, and other local pilots fly mercy missions. The South Dakota National Guard brings in snowplows and M-29 cargo carriers called "weasels" to rescue people and provide supplies. Civilians and military use bulldozers and amphibious vehicles to clear snow.

THE RED CROSS COURIER

MARCH 1949

Georgia Jipp, 1949

Georgia Jipp and Richard Hanson of Operation Snowbound, 1949

JANUARY 11

Another major blizzard strikes. The United States Air Force launches "Operation Haylift" using C-47 and C-48 cargo planes to drop tons of supplies for families and bales of hay for livestock. Two to three major blizzards follow across a wide area, including South Dakota, North Dakota, Wyoming, Nebraska, Utah, Colorado, Arizona, Idaho, Montana, Texas, New Mexico, Nevada, and California. Snow drifts reach fifty feet high. Georgia Jipp begins flying for the Red Cross.

JANUARY 24

President Harry Truman orders "Operation Snowbound." The United States Army, Air Force, and Navy, the American Red Cross, and the Civil Air Patrol clear snow and drop tons of provisions. Millions of sheep and cattle are saved.

MARCH 15

Operation Snowbound ends.

MARCH 30

Winter deals its final blow with another snowstorm. The winter of 1948–1949 ranks among the harshest on record. The disaster area covers 193,000 square miles and affects 1.2 million people. Georgia flew 150 mercy missions for the Red Cross.

❄ 1950 ❄

Georgia writes letters to a newspaper editor and her congressman stating that there are too many regulations for pilots; the congressman discusses her letter in a special hearing in Washington, D.C. Georgia flies stunts at the annual Flying Funfest air show in Philip in front of about two thousand people.

❄ 1951 ❄

The Jipps sail from San Francisco to Honolulu, Hawaii, where Georgia works as a meteorological aide.

❄ 1952–1954 ❄

Georgia attends meteorology schools in Tucson, Arizona, and Oregon State University in Corvallis. She will work a total of 33 years for the United States Weather Bureau in various locations.

❄ 1956–1958 ❄

Georgia works for the United States Weather Bureau in Rapid City, South Dakota.

❄ 1958 ❄

Georgia divorces Richard Jipp. She transfers to the United States Weather Bureau in Lander, Wyoming.

❄ 1960 ❄

Georgia marries Charles Lester Fike in Lander, Wyoming.

❄ 1987 ❄

Georgia Fike dies in Sheridan, Wyoming, at age 60 on April 6. She is buried in Mountain View Cemetery, Riverton, Wyoming.

Meteorologist Georgia Jipp, United States Weather Bureau, Rapid City, S.Dak., mid-1950s

FURTHER READING

Bass, Beverley, and Cynthia Williams. *Me and the Sky: Captain Beverley Bass, Pioneering Pilot*. New York: Alfred A. Knopf, 2019.

Bissonette, Aimee. *Aim for the Skies: Jerrie Mock and Joan Merriam Smith's Race to Complete Amelia Earhart's Quest*. Ann Arbor, Mich.: Sleeping Bear Press, 2018.

Dal Corso, Mara. *Amelia Who Could Fly*. San Diego: Kane Miller/EDC Publishing, 2017.

Engle, Margarita. *The Flying Girl: How Aida de Acosta Learned to Soar*. New York: Atheneum Books for Young Readers, 2018.

Lang, Heather. *Fearless Flyer: Ruth Law and Her Flying Machine*. New York: Calkins Creek, 2016.

Moss, Marissa. *Brave Harriet: The First Woman to Fly the English Channel*. New York: Clarion Books, 2001.

Pimm, Nancy Roe. *Fly, Girl, Fly!: Shaesta Waiz Soars around the World*. Minneapolis: Beaming Books, 2020.

Sandoz, Mari. *Winter Thunder*. Lincoln: University of Nebraska Press, 1986.

SELECTED SOURCES

Alleman, Roy V. *Blizzard 1949*. Grand Island, Neb.: Nebraska Wealth Publishing, 2003.

Dalstrom, Harl A. and Kay Calame. "It's 'Going Down in History': The Blizzards of 1949." *South Dakota History* 29 (Winter 1999): 263–326.

"Flies Mercy Missions." *Miami Daily News*, 2 Feb. 1949.

"January 1949 Blizzard." *National Weather Service*. www.weather.gov/unr/1949-01.

Jipp, Georgia. "Too Many Rules." *Rapid City Journal*, 9 July 1950.

Korson, George. "Operation Snowbound." *American Red Cross Courier* 28 (Mar. 1949): 3–5. Quotation, p. 18.

Murphy, Dorothy Dee. "The West Fights Back." *American Red Cross Courier* 28 (Mar. 1949): 6–9.

Obituary. *Sheridan Press*, 7 Apr. 1987.

"Operation Haylift." www.nebraskastudies.org/en/1925-1949/beef-goes-modern/operationhaylift.

"Our Cover." *Red Cross Courier* 28 (Mar. 1949): [ii]. Quotation, p. 18.

Pfankuch, Bart. "Survivors of Blizzard of 1949 Insist It Was Worst in Region's History." *Rapid City Journal*, 13 Oct. 2013.

"Philip Couple is Married in the Air." *Huron Daily Plainsman*, 21 Oct. 1948.

"Philip Woman Has Flown More Disaster Mercy Missions Than Any Other Pilot." *Deadwood Pioneer Times*, 17 Feb. 1949.

Satzinger, Curt, ed. *First Half Century, Philip, South Dakota, 1907–1957*. Philip, S.Dak.: Pioneer Publishing House, 1957.

"Tailwind Tattler." *Dakota Flyer: The Voice of Dakota Aviation* 3 (Dec. 1948): 5.

"22-year-old Philip Woman Leads State in Storm Mercy Missions." *Huron Daily Plainsman*, 18 Feb. 1949. Quotation, p. 5.

"2000 Attend Philip Air Show Sunday." *Rapid City Daily Journal*, 25 July 1950.

U. S. Congress. House Appropriations. Independent Offices Appropriations for 1951. *Hearings before the Subcommittee of the Committee on Appropriations, House of Representatives*. 88 Cong., 2d sess. (Washington, D.C.: Government Printing Office, 1950).

Velder, Tim. "Etched in Snow: Memories of 1949 Blizzards Still Vivid for Locals." *Rapid City Journal*, 29 Jan. 2009.

"Woman Pilot in Storm Area." *Saint Louis Post-Dispatch*, 2 Feb. 1949.